My Two
Blankets

To my children Nick, Sasha, Matthias, and especially Anna
and her friend Atong, who were the inspiration for this story.

To all the "Cartwheels" of this world, past, present and future
—may you find comfort and understanding in these pages.

Never give up; make your blanket grow! —I.K.

For Alyson O'Brien, who believed in this story from
the beginning. —F.B.

Text copyright © 2014 by Irena Kobald
Illustrations copyright © 2014 by Freya Blackwood

First published in Australia in 2014 by Little Hare Books,
an imprint of Hardie Grant Egmont.

www.hmhco.com

The text of this book is set in Cg Souvenir.
The illustrations are created with a combination of watercolor and oil paints on
watercolor paper.

ISBN 978-0-544-43228-4

Manufactured in China
10 9 8 7 6 5 4 3 2 1
4500476922

My Two Blankets

Irena Kobald & Freya Blackwood

Houghton Mifflin Harcourt

Boston   New York

Auntie used to call me Cartwheel.

Then came the war.

Auntie didn't call me Cartwheel anymore.

We came to this country to be safe.
Everything was strange.
The people were strange.

The food was strange.
The animals and the plants were strange.
Even the wind felt strange.

Nobody spoke like I did.

When I went out, it was like standing
under a waterfall of strange sounds.
The waterfall was cold.
It made me feel alone.

I felt like I wasn't me anymore.

When I was at home,
I wrapped myself in a blanket
of my own words and sounds.
I called it my old blanket.

My old blanket was warm.
It was soft. It covered me all over.
It made me feel safe.
Sometimes I didn't want to go out.
I wanted to stay under my
old blanket forever.

One day a girl in the park smiled at me.
Then she waved.

I wanted to smile back,
but I was scared.

I kept walking with Auntie.

When I looked back,
the girl waved again.

Next time we went to the park, I looked for the girl.
She wasn't there.

We went back three times before I saw her again.
She waved and smiled, and I felt warm inside.

The girl came up to us and said something.
Her words were strange.
It was like being back under
the cold waterfall.

But the girl kept smiling.
She took me to the swings.

I got on and she pushed me
higher and higher.
I wanted to laugh.
I wanted to tell her how glad I was
that we were friends.

But I didn't know how.

When I went home,
I hid under my old blanket.
I wondered if I would
always feel sad.

I wondered if I would
ever feel like me again.

The next time I saw the girl,
she brought some words for me.

She made me say them over and over.

Every time I met the girl,
she brought more words.
Some of the words were hard.
Some of them were easy.

Sometimes I sounded funny
and we laughed.
Sometimes I felt silly
and I wanted to cry.

At night, when I lay in bed
under my old blanket,
I whispered the new words
again and again.

Soon they didn't sound so cold
and sharp anymore.
They started to sound warm and soft.
I was weaving a new blanket.

At first my new blanket was thin and small.
But every day I added new words to it.

The blanket grew and grew.
I forgot about the cold
and lonely waterfall.

My new blanket grew just as
warm and soft and comfortable
as my old blanket.

And now, no matter
which blanket I use,

I will always be me.